# Dawn Light

The **My Magical Pony** series:

Other series by Jenny Oldfield:

# My Magical Pony

## Dawn Light

By Jenny Oldfield

Illustrated by Alasdair Bright

Hodder
Children's
Books

A division of Hachette Children's Books

Text copyright © 2006 Jenny Oldfield
Illustrations copyright © 2006 Alasdair Bright

First published in Great Britain in 2006
by Hodder Children's Books

This edition published in 2007 for Index Books Ltd

4

A Catalogue record for this book is available from the British Library

ISBN-10: 0 340 91078 X
ISBN-13: 9780340910788

Printed and bound in Denmark by Nørhaven Paperback A/S

The paper and board used in this paperback by Hodder Children's Books are
natural recyclable products made from wood grown in sustainable forests. The
manufacturing processes conform to the environmental
regulations of the country of origin.

Hodder Children's Books
A division of Hachette Children's Books
338 Euston Road, London NW1 3BH

# Chapter One

A swallow flew swift as an arrow past Krista's window. She watched it speed on over the rooftop, across the wide moors.

"Breakfast!" her mum called.

Already up and dressed in jeans and sweatshirt, Krista dashed downstairs, gobbled her cereal then headed for the door.

"Brush teeth!" her mum reminded her.

*Rats!* Up to the bathroom, squeeze toothpaste, brush-brush up and down, side to side and back downstairs.

"Bye, Krista!" her mum called. "Have a good day!"

"Ready?" her dad asked. He was waiting in the car.

Krista jumped in. "Oops, no!" Just in time she remembered Spike. Her pet hedgehog needed his morning saucer of milk.

"Hurry up," her dad sighed, tapping the steering-wheel. "I'm going to be late for work."

She jumped out of the car and sped round the back of the house.

"It's OK, I'll look after Spike," her mum said through the kitchen window.

*Phew!* Krista raced back to the car. "Thanks for waiting," she told her dad.

# Dawn Light

As they drove off from High Point down the narrow lane towards town, Krista turned on the radio.

"Sunshine and showers over the coast," the local weather man told them, in between songs and traffic news.

Sure enough, there were clouds over the sea, but big patches of blue sky overhead. There was white blossom in the hedges, and pink flowers grew on the grass verges.

Krista's dad turned the car up the lane leading to Hartfell. Krista looked out of the window and saw Apollo in his field with Scottie. The two horses raised their heads and watched the car pass. In the next field, Drifter, Misty and Kiki came trotting to the gate.

Krista sighed with happiness. She couldn't ask for a better place to be.

It was spring bank-holiday and Krista had a whole week off school. If she got her way she would spend every second of it at Hartfell stables.

"Hi Krista!" Jo Weston, the owner, called

as her dad dropped her off in the yard and
drove away. "I might have guessed you'd be
the first one here!"

Krista hummed a tune as she went to
collect head collars from the tack room.

"Can you bring in Kiki and Drifter?" Jo
asked, passing by with a wheelbarrow loaded
with straw. "And when you've done that, we
have to get Apollo ready for the show in
Whitton this afternoon."

"Cool!" Krista grinned. She looked forward
to grooming the grey thoroughbred then
plaiting his mane and tail ready for the trailer.
"Do you think he's going to win the show-
jumping?" she asked before she went to
collect the ponies.

"You bet!" Jo nodded and smiled.

"Can I come to watch?"

"Sure."

"Wow, thanks!" With an extra spring in her step, Krista went out to the field.

The ponies were brushed and saddled, the yard was full of excited riders in their jodhpurs and hard hats when Krista finally found time to fetch Apollo and begin work on him. She tied him up outside his stable and began to brush the dust out of his dappled grey coat.

"Hey Krista, aren't you riding this morning?" Janey Bellwood asked, looking down from her saddle. She held Drifter on a tight rein to stop him from prancing sideways.

"Nope, too much to do!" Krista answered. "We're taking Apollo to Whitton Show!"

"Lucky you," Janey sighed. Then she thought ahead. "Hey, maybe I'll ask Mum to take me!"

"See you there," Krista nodded, changing brushes and working hard on Apollo's coat. Jo's prize-winning horse stood patiently amidst the hustle and bustle.

"Who's riding Misty?" Nathan Steele wanted to know.

"Carrie," Krista answered. She glanced up at Nathan. "You're on Comanche."

"Cool," he nodded, running off to find his pony.

As Jo finished tacking up, she reminded Krista about Apollo's show saddle. "It's in the house, in the cupboard in the back hallway. Can you dig it out for me?"

"No problem!" Krista would wax and polish the saddle until it shone. Then she would make sure that 'Pollo's bridle and bit were spotless too. "See you later!" she called to the group as they set off on their ponies.

"Busy, busy, busy," she sang into the silence after they'd left. Apollo ducked his big grey head and nuzzled her arm.

"I haven't got any treats!" she smiled. "You look really smart, 'Pollo – you know that?"

He nuzzled her again.

"No treats!" she insisted, laughing because she knew the wily horse could smell the packet of Polos in her pocket. At last she gave in, took out the mints and gave him one.

He snaffled it and crunched it between his teeth.

# My Magical Pony

"I'm too soft!" she murmured, standing back and taking a rest.

Yes, the weather forecast had been right, she noticed. Clouds were gathering, a slight drizzle was falling. For a few moments Krista paused to study the sky, hoping for a faint glimmer of silver light which would mean that Shining Star was on his way.

Star was Krista's very own magical pony who flew to find her whenever someone needed help. But today there was no glittering cloud, no beautiful winged pony soaring over the hilltop to find her. So Krista untied Apollo and led him into his stable.

There was still plenty to do to get ready for the show. *Busy-busy!* Krista thought, running to the house for the thoroughbred's posh saddle. *How good is this! How lucky am I!*

"Last to ride in the final jump-off against the clock is Jo Weston on Apollo!"

Krista heard the announcement and leaned forward over the rail to see Jo and Apollo enter the ring. They trotted close by and Jo gave her a brief wave.

"Come on, Apollo!" Krista whispered.

There was only him and one other horse

left in the show-jumping competition.

"He's a beautiful horse, wonderfully turned out!" a nearby spectator commented, and Krista's chest puffed out with pride. All that brushing, polishing, plaiting and bandaging had been worthwhile.

"Come on, 'Pollo!" she said under her breath.

Jo set him towards the first fence, the bell sounded and he was off.

He cleared the first three jumps with ease, going full-pelt at the next water jump then thundering on towards a triple.

"Wow!" Janey squeezed in alongside Krista and watched the horse fly over the bars. "Come on, Apollo!" she yelled, clapping and jumping up and down.

"You can do it!" Krista breathed. His time was fast. He was still clear.

Jo steered him round the far end of the ring and pushed him on towards a high double, then a single, then a wide, high wall. The wall was the last jump.

Krista half closed her eyes, heard Apollo's hooves click the top bricks, looked away then heard the crowd give a roar.

Krista looked back at the jump. The brick had come loose but hadn't toppled. Apollo had won!

Krista jumped up and cheered. She hugged Janey and they ran together to find Jo and Apollo in the back enclosure.

"Well done!" Krista flung her arms around the horse's neck, then helped Jo take off his saddle and throw a light rug over his sweating back.

*Unbelievable!* she thought. She loved 'Pollo to bits, just as she loved every single other horse and pony at Hartfell.

# Dawn Light

"What a great day!" Janey grinned.

"All days are great when there are horses involved!" Krista declared, proudly watching Jo lead Apollo back into the ring to collect his rosette.

"We won!" she cried, bursting in to the kitchen back home. "Apollo came first in the show-jumping. It was so-oo cool!"

Her mum looked up from the letter she was reading at the table. "Well done," she said quietly.

Krista's dad sat opposite her mum, elbows on the table, head hanging forward.

"You should've seen him racing against the clock. He didn't put a foot wrong!"

Krista rushed to the fridge to look for a cold drink. "Everyone cheered him. He was so pleased with himself when he won!"

"Good," her mum murmured, as if she wasn't really listening.

Krista gulped down her drink. "It's so cool!" she cried. "... Mum, Dad?"

Something was wrong. They weren't smiling or asking her questions about the show.

Krista's dad looked up. He took the letter

from her mum and held it up. "Bad news," he said.

Krista felt her stomach churn. She frowned. "Why? What's happened?"

Her mum sighed and rubbed her forehead as if she had a headache.

"This is a letter from my boss," her dad explained quietly. "It tells me officially that, as from today, I've no job to go to."

Krista stared. "You've lost your job? That's awful!"

He nodded. "I've been expecting it. The firm hasn't been doing too well lately."

Sitting at the end of the table, Krista was lost for words. She looked at her mum. "What happens now?" she asked.

23

"What happens now is that we lose everything we've worked for," her mum said in a flat voice. "Without your dad's salary we can't afford to pay the bills on this place. We'll have to pack up and move."

"We have to leave High Point Farm?" Krista gasped. "We can't do that!"

Slowly her dad nodded. "I'm sorry, love, but that's the way it is. No job – no salary – no house. Full stop."

## Chapter Two

The next morning Krista's dad didn't go into work, so it was her mum who drove her to Hartfell.

"Don't worry, love. Everything will work out OK," her mum promised. "Your dad will find another job."

Krista nodded. "Let's hope," she sighed, saying goodbye to her mum and setting about bringing the ponies in from the fields.

*OK, so we have to leave High Point,* she thought, striding through the rough grass at the edge of the field, calling for Comanche.

*I'm going to hate that, but it's not the end of the world.*

The piebald pony trotted up and poked his nose into the head collar.

She smiled and patted his neck. "You're so good!" she told him, fastening the buckle and leading him out of the field.

*I'll get used to living somewhere different,* she told herself. *But I'll still have the same school, and best of*

*all, I'll still be able to come to Hartfell to help Jo out!*

"Hi!" Jo gave Krista her relaxed wave. "Sorry to hear the news about your dad's job. Your mum called last night and told me."

"I know. But Mum says everything will work out," Krista answered as cheerfully as she could. "We'll probably find somewhere to live not too far away – maybe in Whitton or Maythorne!"

Jo stared carefully at Krista, looked as if she was about to say something, then coughed and turned away.

For the next hour Krista was busy preparing the ponies, going through the routine of fetching them in, grooming them and tacking them up. Soon other riders appeared, chatting and looking forward to their trek.

"Jo and Apollo got first prize in the show-jumping!" Janey told Carrie. "You should have seen 'Pollo fly over the jumps!"

Carrie told everyone about her new pair of riding boots. Nathan arrived late in his dad's new Toyota four wheel drive.

"Who would you like to ride today?" Jo asked Krista.

She ran through the ponies on the list. Would it be willing little Comanche with his shuffling stride, or dainty Misty who would high-step her way to the front? Then there was Shandy, who was always good fun, or Kiki, the three year old light bay who recently arrived and hadn't been ridden much yet. "Hmm, Kiki, please!"

"Good choice." Jo agreed that the newcomer would keep Krista on her toes. She fetched Kiki's saddle and watched as Krista tacked her up. "Why not lead the ride?" she offered.

Springing into the saddle, Krista steered Kiki through the group of riders. "Beach or cliff path?" she asked Jo.

"You choose!"

So Krista led off out of the yard, heading for the cliff path. The others followed in single file, chatting and joking as they went between high hedges and came out on an open track that followed the edge of the cliff which bordered Whitton Bay.

"Hey, Krista, look at the two ships on the horizon!" Carrie called. "One's an oil tanker and the other's a cruise liner!"

Krista stopped to give the ponies a rest. She loved the bird's eye view, realising that they were close to the magic spot where Shining Star would normally appear. The magical pony would call her name and emerge from a shimmering mist, swearing her to secrecy, bringing his wisdom and kindness into her world.

"What are you thinking about?" Carrie broke into Krista's thoughts.

"Oh – nothing!" she laughed. "Just day-dreaming." She glanced down at the bay and then up the heather covered moors to the

# Dawn Light

rocky horizon, knowing that Star would never visit her when others were here. Still she gazed around, looking for tell-tale signs.

"Come on, Krista, let's go!" Nathan yelled from the end of the line. "It's windy. I'm freezing!"

So she led the group on, keeping Kiki on a short rein, looking ahead to make sure there were no dangers on the path that would startle the ponies, so that she could get everyone back safe and sound.

"Krista, would you like a lift home?" Jo offered at the end of a busy day. The yard at Hartfell was empty and everything was tidy, the ponies happily grazing in their fields.

"No, thanks. I'm OK." For once Krista didn't mind the walk along the cliff path. It would give her time to think and rest at the magic spot.

But Jo insisted. "Come on, hop in the Land Rover. I said I'd call in and have tea with your mum anyway!"

So they drove together, with Jo chatting about her plans for Apollo's show-jumping career and Krista happy to stare out of the window at the sheep and wild ponies scattered on the hills.

Soon they arrived at High Point. Krista ran ahead into the house to tell her mum that Jo was here. "Where's Dad?" she asked.

Her mum switched on the kettle. "He's gone to see someone about a new job. He won't be back till late."

"Cool." Krista spooned some cat food into a saucer and went into the back garden to feed Spike, rattling the saucer with the spoon to attract his attention.

Straight away the hungry hedgehog scuttled out of the undergrowth and waddled up to eat his tea.

"Dad's looking for a new job," she told him. "OK, so you don't actually care about stuff like that, Spike. But I can tell Mum's worried, even though she's not saying much."

Spike gobbled noisily, nosing the food off

the saucer and making a thorough mess of his meal.

"It looks like we'll have to leave High Point," Krista sighed. She stopped and gasped. "Oh, I just realised – we might not be able to take you with us!"

She worked it out in her mind. After all, Spike wasn't really a pet. He was a wild animal with his own territory marked out along worn pathways in the hedgerow and ditches. He'd be lost if they took him away from his home ground. "Oh, that's awful!" she cried, jumping to her feet and running back inside. *We can't leave!* she was going to tell her mum. *We have to stay here because of Spike!*

Jo and Krista's mum were so busy talking that they didn't hear her come in.

"This house is much too expensive to keep on," her mum was saying. "I'm going to be sad to leave it, but at the end of the day, what choice do we have?"

"It's tough," Jo agreed. "And, let's face it, Ruth, it's going to be especially hard for Krista."

Krista paused in the kitchen doorway, caught between bursting in and telling her mum they couldn't possibly leave because of Spike, and staying hidden to eavesdrop.

"Yes, she loves it here," her mum agreed. "And I don't think she's fully realised what's happening yet."

Jo nodded. "She seemed to think you could stay around here – maybe find a house in Whitton or somewhere."

Krista held her breath and stayed where she was.

## Dawn Light

"I know," her mum went on. "But that's not likely, I'm afraid. For instance, this job Chris has gone to look at today – it's in Bristol!"

"Which is miles and miles away," Jo murmured. "She's going to be heartbroken if she has to move away from here, into the middle of a big city."

There was a long pause. Krista felt her heart thump against her ribs.

Her mum sighed and got up from the table. "I know she is. But we have to go where the work is. And if it's Bristol, that's just the way it is. There's absolutely nothing anyone can do!"

# Chapter Three

Krista ran upstairs and flung herself on the bed. She buried her face in her pillow, blocked her ears with her hands, tried to un-hear what her mother had just said.

*We can't leave Whitton!* she said to herself. *I have to stay here!*

Leaving would mean saying goodbye to a life she loved. There would be no more Hartfell, no more friends who lived to ride, and worst of all, no more ponies!

No, she couldn't go and live in a city. For a start, what would Jo do without her help?

# Dawn Light

Who would bring the ponies in from the fields during the school holidays and at weekends? Who would muck out the stables during the winter months? Who would clean the tack and make sure that every bridle hung from its proper hook, that every saddle was polished and in its right place?

Then there was Comanche, Kiki, Misty, Shandy and all the rest. The ponies were her life and she was part of theirs. *They'll miss me!* she told herself. *They'll come to the gate each morning to find me and they won't know where I've gone!*

"Krista?" her mum said gently. She'd said goodbye to Jo and come straight upstairs. "Listen to me, love. Try not to be too upset."

Krista kept her face hidden.

"It's not the end of the world."

*It is for me!* she thought. *I don't want to leave. Please don't make me!*

"Krista, look at me." Coming to sit on the edge of her bed, her mum tried hard to be calm. "Nothing's decided yet, so it's silly to get too upset."

# Dawn Light

Krista choked back the sobs that were rising from her chest. There was a glimmer of hope after all, so she turned her face towards her mum. "If nothing's decided, does that mean that we might be able to stay here?"

There was a silence, then her mum shook her head. "No, I'm afraid not, love. I didn't mean that. What I meant was, we've no idea where we'll end up."

"Why not here?" Krista demanded. Didn't her mum understand? She would give any-thing – *anything* – to stay!

"It's to do with your father's job," her mum explained. "There are only a few firms in the country that need someone with his expertise, and they're scattered all over the place ..."

Krista shook her head. She didn't understand or care what her mum was talking about. All she knew was, they couldn't stay in Whitton.

So her mum left her and went downstairs sighing and shaking her head, worried about Krista but realising there was nothing she could say right now that would help.

For a while Krista turned her face back into the pillow and let the muffled sobs come. Then, after she'd cried for a while, she felt better and was able to dry her eyes. *OK, if Mum and Dad won't stay, maybe I could stop with Jo at Hartfell,* she told herself. *I could still go to school and keep my friends. And I'd be on the spot to help at the stables!*

# Dawn Light

Problem solved!

*Oh, but when would I see Mum and Dad? Would they come back to Whitton and visit me? Would they miss me? Would I miss them?*

Krista's bottom lip began to quiver and the tears rose again. Problem not solved after all!

Restlessly she paced the floor until the sound of a car turning into the yard drew her to the window and she saw her dad park and walk quickly towards the house.

She heard him come in and close the front door. She held her breath and crept to the head of the stairs, hanging over the banister to listen in on her parents' conversation.

"Are you tired?" her mum asked.

"Worn out. It was a long drive."

"Have a cuppa."

Krista heard the sound of the kettle being filled and the scrape of a chair across the kitchen floor.

"Well – how did you get on?" her mum asked. "Did they give you the job?"

*Say they didn't!* Krista prayed. *Say we don't have to go to live in a big city away from the ponies!*

Downstairs the silence seemed to last for ever.

"The guy who interviewed me liked me," her dad said at last, his voice filled with relief. "He said I could start work next Monday!"

Wednesday, Thursday, Friday, Saturday, Sunday.

Though she should have been in bed and

fast asleep, Krista counted the days on the calendar on her dressing-table. Only five days left!

"Look on the bright side!" her dad had said when they'd called her down to the kitchen and broken the news. "Remember this is a much better job for me. It means we'll have more money. And we'll find you a good school. You'll soon make new friends and you'll never look back!"

Krista hadn't replied.

"It's been a big shock for her," her mum had explained. "She needs a bit of time to get used to the changes."

The only good thing that had come out of the worst day of Krista's life was that her mum and dad had rung Jo and asked if Krista could stay at Hartfell for the rest of the week while they went to Bristol and looked for a house to rent. Jo had said yes, and so Krista was to spend her last days in Whitton at the place she loved best.

But now, as she tore off the page on her calendar that said Tuesday and she counted the days she had left, her heart sank once more.

Five more times she would take out the head collar and lead Comanche out of the field. Five times she would fetch Misty's saddle and tack her up. She would ride out on five more treks along the lanes, down to the beach, along the cliff path. And then it would be over.

# Dawn Light

*

"Don't worry, I'll take good care of her,"
Jo promised Krista's mum and dad when
they dropped her off at Hartfell early next
morning.

Jo's black cats, Lucy and Holly, came up
and rubbed themselves against Krista's legs.

"Chin up!" Krista's dad told her as he
turned the car in the yard.

"We'll ring you as soon as we have any
news," her mum promised.

They both waved and then the car drove
off.

Jo took Krista upstairs and showed her the
guest room. "Do you mind the cats sleeping at
the bottom of your bed?" she asked.

# My Magical Pony

Krista shook her head.

"They'll be company for you," Jo said with
a smile, pointing out the shower and toilet
opposite Krista's bedroom and telling her that
she would get a great view of the ponies'
fields out of her window.

Krista put her bag on the bed. She took
out her jodhpurs and boots. If there were
only five days left with the ponies, she
was determined to spend every moment
with them.

## Chapter Four

"We heard what happened." Janey came up to Krista soon after she arrived. "I'm really sorry you have to leave!"

"Thanks." Krista nodded but didn't stop grooming Kiki.

The little bay pony had been brushed until her pale coffee coat shone and her dark mane and tail were soft and silky.

"Mum says you can come and stay with us during the holidays any time you like," Janey assured her.

Krista gave another nod and a faint, "Thanks."

"I know it wouldn't be the same as actually living here," Janey went on with tears in her eyes. "But if I had to leave, I'd want to know there was some way I could come back for visits!"

Carrie said the same when she too heard the news. Nathan said he was sorry she was leaving.

All morning Jo kept an eye on Krista, giving her jobs to keep her busy and riding alongside her on Apollo when they went down to the beach for a gallop. "It's tough, huh?" she asked when they'd got back to the yard and the others had gone home for lunch.

Krista nodded. "Everyone's being really nice," she murmured.

# Dawn Light

"Which makes leaving even harder." Jo smiled sadly, resting against the tack room wall, hands in pockets and looking up at the light clouds scudding across the sky. "I've always thought goodbye was the hardest word in the English language," she added softly.

Harder even than Krista had imagined when she'd first heard the news about her dad's job. It was as if she wanted to hang on to every minute of the day.

But the clock ticked, and soon it would be four more days and then three ...

Krista spent the afternoon working with Kiki in the paddock, training the little three-year-old to change leads and keep her balance as she cantered round corners. They concentrated hard and for a while Krista almost forgot her worries. At the end of the training session she rewarded Kiki with a Polo from her pocket.

"I saw that!" Jo called from a distance, pretending to tell Krista off for sneaking the treat on the sly. "Now they'll all expect a mint every time they work hard!"

Blushing, Krista led Kiki into her stable. She was halfway through taking off her tack when she suddenly remembered Spike.

"I forgot – I have to go home to feed my hedgehog!" she told Jo, hurriedly handing over the bay pony and setting off at a run across the yard. He hadn't had any breakfast, he would be starving hungry.

"How long will you be?" Jo called after her.

"An hour," Krista promised. "I'll go by the
cliff path – it's quickest!"

She ran down the lane, jumped the stile
and sprinted on along the sandy path towards
High Point. How could she have forgotten
poor Spike?

The little hedgehog was waiting for Krista on
the back lawn. She took him his saucer of
food and a bowl of milk and put them on the
ground side by side.

"Sorry!" she told him.

He waded into the middle of the dish
of milk, put his sharp snout into the saucer of

meat and gobbled hungrily. When he'd
finished his food he paddled backwards and
shook himself dry.

"Oh, Spike!" Krista said softly. The sight of
him licking his little black paws almost made
her cry. "Whatever are we going to do?"

Spike shook himself some more, then set off at a smart trot across the lawn. *I don't know about you, but I'm off looking for a nice deep ditch to roll in!* He vanished quickly under the hedge and left Krista sitting alone in the evening sun.

She sighed, collected the dishes, took them into the house and made sure that it was locked. Then she set off for Hartfell.

*I mean it – what are we going to do?* she said to herself, retracing her steps along the cliff path. *Who will feed Spike after I'm gone?*

Krista was so wrapped up in her sad thoughts that she didn't notice when she approached the magic spot. And she didn't look up at the one white cloud that split off

from the bank of clouds hanging low over
the watery horizon, drifting towards her,
growing larger as it came.

*Spike will never be able to look after himself!* she
thought. *He needs me!*

The cloud floated over Whitton Bay.
It cast a light shadow over the beach and
then the sheer cliff rising from it. As it drew
near to the place where Krista walked, it
seemed to glitter.

"Krista!" a voice murmured, soft as the wind.

She walked on without looking up.

Shining Star said her name a second time.
"Krista!"

*Jo was right – goodbye is the hardest word!* she
thought.

## Dawn Light

The magical pony looked down on her from his shimmering silver cloud. "This is strange!" he murmured. "Krista is wrapped in sorrow, yet she does not look for me!"

She walked straight on, past the magic spot.

Shining Star beat his great white wings and waited.

*

*It's hopeless!* Krista thought. The more she tried to find an answer to her problems, the worse they seemed to be.

In less than a week she would be gone. There would be no more High Point, no more Hartfell. Instead, there would be strangers in a strange city.

Shining Star hovered over the magic spot. He watched carefully, wondering what was wrong, hearing a mysterious sound of roaring engines, seeing shadowy crowds surrounded by tall buildings made of glass and concrete. *Krista is going away!* he realised.

He saw her reach the end of the cliff path and hesitate.

# Dawn Light

Before she climbed the stile into the lane, Krista glanced up at the moors. The sun had gone down and the hillside was in deep shadow, the sky over the western sea turning from pinkish gold to deep red.

Shining Star saw her turn towards the moors and then the shimmering water. "Krista!" he called her back.

This time she heard. She recognised his voice and looked for him in the low cloud over the moor.

Yes, the drifting cloud shone silver. Glittering droplets fell to the ground.

"Tell me your trouble," Star whispered.

For a few moments Krista was drawn back to the magic spot. She climbed down from the stile and took a few steps towards Shining Star, looking for his shape within the mist, waiting for him emerge.

But then she stopped. So, her magical pony was here and she could pour her heart out to him, tell him all her troubles. But then what?

And surely Star's job was to save people and creatures in danger. *I'm not in danger*, she reminded herself. *And I don't think I can bear to tell him my news.*

"Come!" Shining Star urged. He beat his wings gently. "Speak to me!"

Krista shook her head and let out a deep sigh. No, she hadn't the heart. Sadly she turned back towards Hartfell.

## Dawn Light

Shining Star watched in silence. He beat his wings and rose higher in the evening sky. When he was sure that Krista would not return, he turned towards the sunset and flew away.

## Chapter Five

Next day Krista woke early to find Lucy and Holly curled up asleep at the foot of her bed.

For a moment, she wondered where she was, then her head cleared and everything rushed back. She was in Jo's guest room with its pale yellow walls and white curtains, tucked under a soft cream duvet with two black cats sleeping soundly at her feet. It was Thursday, and last night she'd turned down the chance to go and meet her magical pony!

# Dawn Light

Krista's heart skipped a beat. *I should have spoken to him!* she sighed. *I should at least have said goodbye!*

Goodbye to Shining Star, the amazing glittering pony with his wonderful white flowing mane and proud head. Would she ever see him again?

Together they had helped farmers and friends all around Whitton – ponies trapped by the tides, kids with heartaches – and Star's magic had worked every time.

But no more. Unless … A sudden thought struck Krista and she slid quickly out of bed. Unless Shining Star had appeared last night because someone else was in danger and he needed her help!

She put on her jeans and T-shirt, socks and riding boots, intending to run to the magic spot and wait for Star to return. At the end of her bed, the two cats woke up and stretched.

"Morning, Krista!" Jo called up the stairs. "You're up early. Would you like bacon and eggs?"

Krista groaned. She realised she would have to stay to eat breakfast. And then the day's routines would begin – bringing in the ponies from the fields, getting ready for lessons and treks, grooming, cleaning, sweeping and mucking-out. With all this going on, she wouldn't be able to get away.

Downstairs Jo greeted her with a plate stacked high with food, and lots of cheerful talk about the day ahead. "The blacksmith is coming to put shoes on Scottie and Apollo, and at some point I have to drive the Land Rover in for its MOT. I'll probably take the trailer into town at the same time and buy a load of supplies."

Krista ate slowly, sorely regretting that she'd turned her back on her magical pony and wondering how she could put it right.

Then the phone rang and it turned out to be Krista's mum calling from Bristol.

"Hello, love. How are you doing?"

"Fine," Krista replied untruthfully.

"We're getting on well here," her mum reported. "We've been looking at some nice houses near to where Dad will be working, though we haven't fixed on one yet. Today we'll find out about the schools in the area."

"Cool," she said in a flat voice. To her it didn't seem real — more like a bad dream that she would soon wake up from.

"You're sure you're OK?" her mum checked.

"Sure," Krista insisted. "Listen, Mum, I'm busy. I've got to go and bring in the ponies. See you soon. Bye!"

\*

# Dawn Light

Busy was best, Krista decided, even though there was no chance of getting away to visit the magic spot.

At Hartfell there was always loads to do. A pony would need to be groomed and tacked up, a rider would be asking questions – "Are my stirrups the right length?", "Is my girth tight enough?", "Has anyone seen my hard hat?"

All morning she went about her usual business, but her face was sad and there was no spring in her stride. Janey, Carrie and the others understood, and even the horses seemed to sense that something was wrong. Every time she went near Comanche, he stuck his big brown and white face close to hers, as if to say, "What's up? Why the sad face?" And Misty didn't fidget as usual when Krista was putting on her saddle, seemingly aware that Krista was having a hard day.

"These ponies pick up on people's moods," Jo commented when she and Krista took a break for lunch. "I saw Shandy giving you a little nudge with her nose, saying 'Hey, cheer up!'"

"Yeah," Krista sighed. "Sorry!"

"Don't apologise!" Jo said. "We're all in the same boat – moping around because we're sorry to see you go!"

The afternoon was the same – Krista got through a thousand jobs, rushing from one to the next so the sad thoughts couldn't hijack her. She lifted and carried, brushed and shovelled, until by teatime she was exhausted.

"Sit!" Jo ordered Krista into the house. "Watch TV, chill out!"

Krista dragged herself inside on weary legs then flopped down on a chair in the living room. As soon as she sat, the sadness came back in a rush.

"Oh no!" Krista couldn't bear the thoughts that crowded in – Thursday was gone; only three days to go, then two, then one, and nothing would stop the march of time, not even Shining Star's powerful magic!

*Shining Star!* Krista stood up and went to the window. *He came and I didn't go to meet him! But who knows – maybe he'll come back!*

.She jumped up from the chair and dashed
outside.

"I thought I told you to take it easy!" Jo
warned, resting her sweeping brush against a
stable door.

"I will when I've fed Spike!" Krista used
a good excuse to get away to the magic spot
at last.

# Dawn Light

"Take Comanche," Jo told her. "He's still tacked up and he'll get you there and back in half the time."

She nodded. With Comanche she would take the bridleway leading to the cliff path. They would stop and look for Shining Star, and with luck she would still have time to get over to High Point and back before dusk.

The willing piebald stood patiently as Krista put her foot in the stirrup and mounted. He set off briskly out of the yard, happy to be out and about.

"You never know, Comanche," Krista muttered as she rode along. "Star might come back and give me something important to do before I leave!"

# My Magical Pony

The pony's hooves clip-clopped up the lane.

"I wonder what he wanted," Krista went on. "He never comes unless someone is in trouble."

Comanche enjoyed the sound of his rider's soft voice. He flicked his ears towards her as if understanding every word.

Krista turned the sturdy pony on to the cliff path and looked ahead into the distance. Tall ferns grew at the edge of the cliff, with yellow gorse bushes half-hiding a barbed wire fence.

# Dawn Light

Beyond the rickety fence there was a sheer drop to the sea below.

"There's no sign of Star so far," she murmured.

They drew closer to the magic spot – a place on the path which she recognised by a sudden hollow and a flat, sandy patch of ground. Overhead, the sky was clear and still.

Comanche picked up his broad hooves and crunched them down on the sandy track. His thick white tail swished away troublesome flies.

"Whoa!" Krista pulled on the reins as they drew near the magic spot. She longed to see the magical cloud and to feel a gust of warm, swirling wind.

## My Magical Pony

*Why did I ignore him last night?* she asked
herself glumly, for Shining Star gave no sign
that he was near.

Comanche shifted restlessly. He tugged at
the reins and stamped his feet.

Alone on the cliff path, Krista gazed down
at the bay. Everything was calm and she began
to feel certain that her magical pony wouldn't
come. "We'll wait a bit longer!" she whispered
to Comanche, hoping against hope.

They stood on the edge of the cliff, where
the land met the sea, watching and listening.

"No!" Krista said at last, feeling sadder
than ever. "Last time Star came I let him
down. I disappointed him. Now he'll never
come again!"

## Chapter Six

Far away, in a land beyond the stars, where darkness never fell, Shining Star was with his sister, Pale Moon. They stood at ease in a meadow of feathery grass and a million tiny white flowers.

"Tell me again about the girl, Krista," Pale Moon said, her white wings folded at her sides. She too was surrounded by a glittering mist. Her face was gentler than Shining Star's, and less proud.

"I flew to her world because she is sad," Star began. "Many times Krista has helped me, and now I want to come to her aid. But she did not answer me."

"Are you sure she heard you?" Pale Moon inquired.

Star nodded.

"That is strange." Pale Moon stood for a while in thought. "What is the cause of Krista's sadness?" she asked.

Shining Star shook his head. "She has not told me, but in her mind I see tall buildings and many crowded streets."

Pale Moon cocked her head to one side. "But you see no horses?"

"No."

"Then that is the reason for her sorrow," Shining Star's sister concluded. "But unless she

comes to you and asks for your help, there is
no magic you can use, there is no comfort
you can give her."

In the world below, while the magical ponies
rested and talked, Krista and Comanche had
arrived at the magic spot.

In Galishe, meanwhile, North Star flew to
join Shining Star and Pale Moon. He trailed a
cloud of silver mist behind him, his wings
made a strong breeze that rippled through the
long grass.

North Star landed beside his brother and
sister. "You have had your rest and now you
must come with me," he ordered. "Our magic
is needed in a land far from here."

# Dawn Light

Straight away Shining Star and Pale Moon spread their wings ready for flight.

Together with their older brother, North Star, they would fly far away.

The three magical ponies rose into the clear, bright air. Their wings were broad and strong, the light from their pure white coats glowed silver. They flew high into the sky above Galishe towards the neighbouring world.

Far below, Krista called for Shining Star, but he did not hear.

Friday morning broke dull and cloudy. Jo was up early, preparing to take Apollo in the trailer to a jumping lesson with Adam Letts, one of the top trainers in the county.

"I'll be gone all day," she told Krista. "But Rob Buckley is coming to help out here. You know Rob?"

Krista nodded. On any other day she would have asked if she could go with Jo and Apollo to watch their lesson and learn lots of new tips from the great Adam Letts, but today was different. Today was Day Three in the countdown to leaving Hartfell for ever.

"Rob will need lots of advice from you," Jo told Krista. "I hope you don't mind."

"No problem," Krista said, remembering her motto that busy was best. She helped Jo get Apollo ready for the trailer, then, when Rob arrived, she volunteered to

# Dawn Light

bring in the ponies as usual.

"You're the boss!" Rob grinned at her.
"I'll just do as I'm told."

Krista smiled back. She liked Rob because
he was easy-going and jokey. She would enjoy
working with him. "OK, you get to work with
the brushes," she told him. "These ponies have
to look good before their riders arrive."

"Bring them in!" he answered, rolling up his
sleeves. He began to whistle and work, and
didn't stop until Scottie, Kiki, Shandy, Drifter,
Comanche and Misty were spotless.

"Saddles!" Krista said next.

Out came the leather wax and cloths.
Together Krista and Rob polished until their
arms ached.

"Bridles!"

More rubbing and polishing. "Phew!" Rob muttered. "I never knew running a riding school was such hard work!"

They were ready just in time. As they tacked up their last pony, Nathan arrived. Soon the yard was full of eager riders.

"Hi everyone, this is Rob." Krista introduced him as he saddled Scottie, the chestnut ex-racehorse. "He'll be leading this morning's ride."

"No, he won't!" Rob argued, settling into the saddle and turning towards Krista who was riding Misty. "Hey, I'm just the hired help. Krista, you're the boss. Why don't you lead us?"

She grinned and nodded. "OK, where does everyone want to go?"

"The beach!" someone said.

"The cliff path!"

"Let's go somewhere new!"

"Well, boss?" Rob asked.

"We'll try the bridle track up on to the moor top," she decided, her spirits raised by Rob. "We haven't been there for a while."

"Cool!" Nathan said. "I like it up there."

And so they set off, full of chatter, the ponies striding out up the hill,

the breeze catching them as they reached the summit and looked back down over the moors.

Far above, Shining Star flew from distant Galishe, his work finished. He sped between the planets and stars, intent on visiting Krista to see how she fared.

He reached Whitton Bay at the time when Krista led her ride on to the moors. Watching from a distance, hidden by his magical cloud, he saw a single file of riders and ponies make their way to the top of the hill. He heard the chatter and laughter, saw a smile light up Krista's face.

*This is good, he* thought.

## Dawn Light

He observed her riding her grey pony, picking her way along the winding moorland track, calling out to other riders to take care.

Her voice carried in the wind. She sounded happy.

*Krista has forgotten her sorrow*, Shining Star said to himself. *I am glad.*

Reassured, the magical pony watched a while longer. Then, thinking that Krista's troubles were over, he beat his wings and flew away.

## Chapter Seven

"You did a great job," Rob told Krista after she'd led the morning ride. They were taking a lunch break, sitting on straw bales in the barn to shelter from a chilly wind.

"Thanks." She blushed and bit into her cheese sandwich, already thinking about the jobs for the afternoon.

"You must know the bridleways around here like the back of your hand."

Krista nodded.

Rob offered her a packet of crisps. "Jo's lucky to have you around," he commented, tearing open his own bag. "I don't know what she'd do without you."

*Ouch!* Krista pretended to be too busy eating to reply. Obviously Rob hadn't heard the news.

Rob chatted on. "I expect you're hoping to find a job connected with horses when you leave school. Personally I can't picture you wanting to do anything else – for a start, you're a natural horsewoman!"

*Too much!* Krista nearly choked on her crisps. Her good mood of the morning plummeted. "Don't you know?" she muttered.

"Know what?" Rob asked, puzzled.

"My dad lost his job. We have to leave Whitton."

It was Rob's turn to go red and almost choke. "You're kidding!"

Sighing, Krista shook her head then stood up. "No, it's definite. We're moving to live in a city. End of story."

That evening, Krista waited until Jo came back with Apollo before she set off on foot to High Point to feed Spike.

She was worn out as she climbed the stile and took the cliff path, too tired to notice that the grey clouds over the sea were growing darker and moving towards the land. The air grew damp and gloomy.

Almost in a daze by the time she reached home, Krista unlocked the kitchen door and

# Dawn Light

got the hedgehog's tin of food out of the
fridge, scooping it carefully into his special
saucer. Then she took it out to the garden,
rattling the spoon against the saucer to attract
his attention.

"Here, Spike!" she called, expecting the
prickly bundle to emerge from one of the
hedges. "Come on, boy, din-dins!"

# My Magical Pony

Spike didn't appear so Krista set the saucer on the grass and went back inside for his milk. *I expect he's sulking 'cos no one's at home,* she thought. When she came out again she called more loudly.

Still no Spike. Krista felt a small dart of fear inside her chest. "Spike!" she called again. Then she went looking for him in the hedges and in the ditch beside the back lane.

*What if he's been hurt?* she thought. *He could be lying injured where no one can find him!*

The fear grew into a tight band around her chest. Spike never went missing! He always showed up for his dinner! By now Krista was certain that something was wrong.

To make things worse, a steady rain had

begun to fall. As Krista searched the ditch she felt the heavy drops soak through her T-shirt. She went further, into the back lane, across a field towards some trees where Spike might be wandering.

*Maybe he's trapped in a ditch or down a rabbit burrow!* Krista thought. Under the shadow of the trees the light grew fainter, but at least the thick branches held off the rain. "Spike!" she called, stumbling over a thick root and almost falling headlong.

Soon it was too dark to see. Krista knew it was time to retrace her steps towards the field, the lane and the house, but now she wasn't sure which way to go. She turned around on the spot, trying to pick out a landmark to show which way she had come.

*All the trees look the same!* she thought, bumping her head on a low branch and staggering back. She set off in one direction, then stopped and tried another. And every second the woods seemed to get darker and the rain fell more heavily on the canopy of leaves.

Finally she stopped trying to find her way out. It came as a shock to Krista to realise that she was lost. *I know my way!* she told herself. *I've lived here all my life!*

But this was serious. She shook her head and tried to think, remembering that she'd left the kitchen door at High Point standing open, realising too that even if she found her way out of the wood, it would soon be too dark to find the path back to Hartfell.

"I've got to get out of here!" she muttered, setting off again towards a point between the trees that seemed lighter and more open.

Still the rain poured down. Now the tall
trunks seemed to form a passageway for
Krista to go down, offering her a way out.
Quickly she took it and began to run. But was
it a mistake? Was she running towards High
Point or away from it? Her heart thumped as
she hesitated then decided that she had no
choice but to go forward.

She ran on in the darkness, to the edge of
the wood. Then she left the trees behind and
came into the open, into the downpour and
gusts of strong wind that blew the rain against
her face.

Krista staggered. She put her hand up
to shield her eyes, feeling the wind cut
through her. Everything was blurred and dark,

# Dawn Light

but she must press forward.

Suddenly the rocky ground fell away.
She slid down a stony surface, flinging her
arms wide to catch hold of any solid object
that would halt her fall. Her fingers grasped
at a low, thorny bush. They closed around a
thin branch and she stopped.

Catching her breath, Krista felt for a
foothold. She heard stones loosen underfoot
and listened to them roll and then fall over
an unseen edge, rattling against rock as they
disappeared.

Then she felt the roots of the bush that
had halted her slide begin to tear and loosen.

Frantically she grabbed with her
other hand for another, sturdier branch,

95

twisting and stretching before the bush gave way. Still the rain battered her, and the wind brought the sound of huge waves crashing against the shore.

*I'm on the edge of the cliff!* she realised.

Horrified, she struggled to stand on the steep, slippery slope. Her hand-hold was tearing loose, roots and all. Her feet couldn't steady her. *I'm falling!* she thought.

Suddenly the weak bush came free and Krista slid. Stones tore at her thin clothes, her bare arms scraped against the rock. And then there was nothing except space and the sound of the waves.

She fell over the cliff into black night.

# Chapter Eight

Rob and Jo stood in the yard at Hartfell.

"Krista's been gone a long time," Jo muttered. She looked up at the gloomy sky, predicting that it would start to rain within half an hour. "At this rate she's going to get drenched!"

"Let's drive over to her place," Rob suggested. "If we get there before she sets off back along the path, we can give her a lift."

"We'd better get a move on," Jo decided, dashing inside for her Land Rover key. "I don't like the idea of her walking back in a downpour!"

They set off down the lane, but by the time they reached the turn-off for High Point, rain had already begun to fall. Jo flicked on the windscreen wipers and the headlights.

"We shouldn't have let her go," Rob reflected. "It was only to feed her hedgehog and she was already worn out, poor kid."

"Yeah, but you try stopping her," Jo argued. "When Krista sets her mind on something, she goes ahead and does it."

"She's a great girl."

Jo nodded thoughtfully. "She doesn't want to leave Whitton."

"I don't blame her. If there's any kid who belongs around horses and puts her heart and soul into them, it's Krista!"

# Dawn Light

They rattled along the lane in silence for a while, splashing through puddles. A high wind blew torrential rain against the screen, making it hard for Jo to see.

"Let's hope she's had the sense to wait inside the house until the rain eases," Rob muttered, growing more concerned as the storm buffeted the Land Rover and thick clouds shrouded the hills in mist.

"We'll soon see," Jo said, driving suddenly off the lane into the yard at High Point. "I nearly missed that turning," she muttered.

Quickly Rob and Jo jumped down from the Land Rover and ran towards the house.

"The front door's open!" Rob pointed out. "It looks like we got here in time."

Jo went into the house. "Krista!" she called.

There was no reply, so Rob took off his wet boots and went upstairs. "Krista?"

"Is she up there?" Jo asked.

"No, there's no sign."

Going through to the kitchen, Jo found that the back door was open too. She went out into the garden and called Krista's name again. Rain swept across the lawn, and it was almost too dark to see. She went back into the kitchen to find Rob

examining an open tin of cat food and the
door key that had been left on the worktop
beside it.

"Why would she leave without locking
up?" he asked.

Jo took a deep breath and tried to figure
it out. "Maybe she was so tired she didn't
know what she was doing. She saw there was
a storm coming and just set off without
remembering to lock the doors."

"That's not like Krista, is it?"

"No," she admitted. "Rob, I've got a bad
feeling—"

"Me too," he cut in. "Listen, I'll scout
around on the lane. You take another look in
the back garden. If we don't find her soon,

I guess we'll have to grab a torch and follow her along the cliff path. With luck, we'll be able to catch up with her."

"OK, hurry!" Jo agreed. This situation was not good. In fact, it was quickly turning into a nightmare. "Krista!" she yelled at the top of her voice, rushing out into the storm.

Krista couldn't hear Rob and Jo's voices calling her name. She didn't see the flash of torchlight along the dark cliff path or feel the force of the wind blowing the storm in from the sea.

She lay at the foot of the cliff without moving, her eyes closed.

Rain swept into the narrow cove where she

had fallen, drenching her. The sea crept up the shore, swirling towards the rocks, but still a safe distance away.

Nothing woke her – not the sound of voices far above nor the crash of waves and the drag of pebbles on the beach. She knew nothing about the continuing storm, lost in her dark, silent world.

In Galishe, Pale Moon stood alone in her field of silvery grass, waiting.

The magical pony was troubled. She heard sounds of the sea – the surge of waves, the rush of wind. They came from far away, from a place she did not recognise.

Then she heard voices calling above the

waves, she saw a beam of yellow light through darkness and rain.

Pale Moon was alert, her ears pricked, looking this way and that across the bright meadow.

*Come home, brothers!* she thought. *Now is*

*not the time to be flying among the stars. Come to me here in Galishe and hear what I can hear!*

The gentle pony waited a long time before North Star and Shining Star returned. They appeared in a shimmering mist that shone gold under a bright sun. Their wings were spread in swift flight.

Pale Moon looked up. "I am glad to see you," she told Shining Star as he landed beside her.

He folded his wings and looked closely at his sister's face. "What troubles you?" he asked.

"Look far," she told him. "Listen!"

Shining Star obeyed. Below the stars, on Earth, there was a black storm. It drove the waves against the rocky shore and brought danger to Krista.

"Do you hear?" Pale Moon asked.

Star nodded. "But Krista does not call me,"
he murmured.

His sister tossed her head. "Perhaps she
cannot call," she pointed out.

"Listen again!" North Star instructed.

The three magical ponies strained to hear
voices through the distant storm, calling
Krista's name.

"Pale Moon is right," North Star decided.
"The girl Krista is in danger!"

Shining Star spread his wings, listening for
more clues. "I hear women crying," he told
them.

"Now, or in the future?" Pale Moon asked

anxiously. She knew that, like all the magical ponies, her brother had the power to visit past, present and future.

"Not now, nor in time to come," he answered quietly, still listening intently. "The women weep long ago. They stand by the shore, looking out to sea. They cling to each other for comfort."

Pale Moon and North Star were intrigued. Surely Shining Star did not have to fly back in time to help the girl.

"Go quickly!" North Star told his brother. "Fly like the wind."

"Yes, go!" Pale Moon echoed.

Shining Star beat his wings and rose from the world of Galishe. He shone as he flew,

# My Magical Pony

like a star through the dark sky, trailing silver
light, falling to Earth.

# Chapter Nine

By midnight, Krista's mum and dad were on their way home from Bristol.

"Something terrible has happened," Jo Weston had told them over the phone. "Krista has gone missing."

Krista's mother had made Jo repeat the message.

"She set off from Hartfell earlier this evening to feed Spike," Jo explained. "She never came back. Rob Buckley and I searched everywhere then we called the police."

Krista's mum had refused to believe the news.

She'd handed the phone to Krista's dad.

"We're in the middle of a bad storm here," Jo had continued. "There's still a chance that Krista's sheltering from the rain somewhere."

"Not at this time of night," Krista's dad had said. "Jo, you're sure you looked everywhere you could think of?"

"Everywhere!" Jo had insisted. "I'm so sorry! You'd better get back here as quick as you can!"

And now they drove along the motorway with fear gripping them, yet trying to find a reason behind their daughter's disappearance.

"Maybe she was picked up by a friend!" In desperation, Krista's dad made her mum call Janey's house.

# Dawn Light

Each time the answer was the same – no one had seen Krista since they'd left the stables at tea time. Everyone would pass on the word that she was lost. In the morning, if Krista was still missing, they would join together and form a local search party.

"Perhaps she was worried about the ponies in the storm," Krista's mum said as they sped towards Whitton. "I wonder if Jo's been out in the fields to look."

She rang again. "Jo, maybe Krista was checking on the ponies and somehow hurt herself and was unable to make it back to the house. Did you look in the fields?"

Ten minutes later Jo called back. "Still no sign of her," she reported. "The police are here, but they say the weather is holding them back. They have to wait until dawn before they can send out a search helicopter."

Krista's mum began to sob. "She's had an accident!" she cried. "Hurry – we have to find her!"

"We will," Krista's dad muttered. "I'm driving as fast as I can!"

They were thirty miles from home when they ran into the storm that was lashing the coast. It was three a.m. and pitch-black. They drove on in terrified silence.

Two women were weeping on the shore. They had lost a loved one on this treacherous coast and their spirits had haunted the place ever since.

Shining Star saw them standing in a narrow cove – one young, one old. They wore dresses that reached the ground and shawls around their shoulders.

*This is long ago,* he told himself, looking down on the coastline. *It is the shore where Krista lives. I see Whitton Bay and the sharp rocks of Black Point. There are sailing ships with great white sails out to sea. In the town the men sell the fish they catch.*

Believing that the mysterious weeping figures might help him in his search for Krista, Star had used his magic to take him back to the time of the women. He had arrived on a winter's day and hovered invisible over their heads.

The young woman stood on a grey pebbled beach, weeping bitter tears in the old woman's arms. Wind blew their long black skirts and made them billow like ships' sails.

*"She will never come back!"* the young woman wept. *"The sea has taken her!"*

*"It is cruel to lose a child!"* the old woman murmured. *"The waves will not return her."*

*"My only child snatched from me!"* the young woman wept. *"Your granddaughter!"*

# Dawn Light

Shining Star hovered and listened. He studied the narrow cove and wondered how this old, ghostly sadness could link with Krista's trouble in the present. He felt certain that the sorrowing women held the key.

*"Come away,"* the grandmother urged. *"The tide has turned. We must leave the shore."*

Still weeping, the young woman turned her back to the sea.

Star watched the women's slow progress between the rocks. He saw them climb rough steps to the cliff path, hindered by their long skirts. They stopped at the top to look down.

*"Gone from this treacherous spot,"* the old woman said sadly. *"A moment's carelessness is enough for a child to slip and fall."*

# My Magical Pony

Shining Star gazed along the cliff and up towards the farm on the hill. *That is High Point, he realised. And now the women make their way through the trees to Krista's house!*

The magical pony understood the women's loss as he silently said farewell to the past and flew through time with a heavy heart. And he knew now why the ancient voices had reached him in Galishe. *They were warning me of the very place where Krista has fallen, like the child long ago!* Shining Star sighed and shook his head. The message was troubling. It filled him with dread.

Towards dawn the storm lifted. The wind blew the clouds northwards. Light broke in the east.

Krista lay on the beach where the girl had

drowned more than a hundred years earlier.
Her eyes were still closed after the long
night. Her face was pale and lifeless.

The sun came up over the hill, bringing
colour back to the moors, casting early
morning shadows.

"... *She will never come back!*" a voice
murmured.

"... *The waves will not return her!*" another whispered.

The sea crept closer to Krista, its white foam licked at her feet.

Krista's eyelids flickered. Her hand twitched.

"... *Come away!*" said the whispering voice. "*The tide has turned. Come away!*"

Shining Star flew from the past into the present. He came to the place where Krista had fallen during the storm.

"... *Cruel!*" the first voice moaned. "... *My only child!*"

As the cold waves washed against Krista in the dawn light, she opened her eyes.

*

# Dawn Light

Car doors slammed in the yard at High Point. Jo and Rob followed Krista's dad and mum inside the house.

"The police can send out their helicopter now that it's light," Rob reported. "They have officers on the ground, searching the cliff path."

"Why would she leave her key?" Krista's mother demanded over and over again.

"Ssshhh!" Krista's dad said gently. He went out of the back door into the garden, where he saw Spike's empty saucers on the grass and almost broke down.

"Everyone is out looking for her." Jo had followed him and stood by his side. She gazed downhill towards the small cluster of twisted, leaning trees.

"Let's hope that we're in time!" he murmured, looking towards the rising sun.

Krista gazed up at the dawn sky. It was calm and pearly grey. She closed her eyes again, drifting away.

The shallow waves washed around her, lapping at her cold body.

Krista gasped and came back to consciousness. She raised her head and saw the pale pebbles on the shore, closed her fingers around their smooth surface, grasped a handful then let them drop.

Struggling to move, Krista rolled away from the water, on to her stomach. She was bruised and stiff. Another wave broke and washed over her.

*What happened? Where am I?* she wondered.

Overhead there was the churning sound of a helicopter engine and the whirr of metal blades. It passed by without stopping.

*There was a storm,* Krista recalled. *I was lost, and then I fell.*

The foaming water made her drag herself up the beach. Every movement was painful; her head swam dizzily. *I'm not going to make it!* she thought.

Shining Star looked down from the cliff top. He saw that the tide was coming in rapidly now, eating up the beach so that there was only a narrow strip of land before the rocks rose sheer to the place where he stood.

# My Magical Pony

At first the magical pony could not spot his young friend, though the ghostly voices which had wakened Krista had led him to this spot. He stared intently down into the shadowy cove, driving the weeping women from his head, concentrating on what he could see in the present moment. "Krista!" he called, spreading his wings and rising from the rocky ground.

*The tide is coming in!* she realised. Another wave broke and she struggled into the shelter

of an overhanging rock. *Even if I found a path
up to the top of the cliff, I'd never have the strength to
climb it!*

Helplessly she collapsed on to the pebbles,
hearing the roar of the waves at her feet,
feeling the icy spray against her skin.

Some way off, over Black Point, the police
helicopter turned and flew back.

Shining Star heard the growl of the engine
growing closer, so he dipped down almost to
sea level and continued his search. Skimming
the waves, sensing that she was very close,
he called Krista's name.

"I won't make it alone!" Krista groaned,
raising her hand to attract the helicopter's
attention.

Blown off course by the whirring blades,
Shining Star was swept close to the rocks.
He beat his wings to fly clear and wait until
the flying machine had passed.

"Help!" Krista called to the pilot. A strong
wave broke against her, almost dragging her
back down the beach as it retreated.

The police crew saw no sign of the lost
girl beneath the overhanging rock. They flew
on towards the next inlet.

Now another wave crashed against Krista,
flinging her on to her back and sucking her
clear of the cliff. Salt water filled her mouth.

Shining Star flew back towards the cove.
He heard Krista's call for help and saw her
now, half floating in the foaming water, one

arm raised. "Hold on!" he called, swooping down, plunging into the sea and swimming strongly towards her.

Krista felt the waves drag her down. She saw Shining Star with his outstretched wings, watched him plummet into the sea and then saw his head rise to the surface. Her heart leaped and she struggled to stay afloat until he reached her.

"Take hold!" he told her, swimming close. "Make haste!"

Krista reached out. She grasped at Star's mane but the strength of the waves carried her away. Once more the sea closed over her head.

Shining Star turned and swam after her.

He dived below the surface, searching for Krista amongst the rocks and weeds.

Under the water she saw his pale shape and began to swim once more, drawing close enough to stretch out again. This time her fingers closed around his flowing mane.

Shining Star waited until Krista had a firm grasp around his neck, then he rose to the surface. They broke clear of the murky water and breathed again.

"Hold tight," he told her.

Krista clasped his strong neck and slid on to his back. She looked towards the shore and saw that the tide had now swallowed up the beach completely, and waves crashed against the cliff.

# Dawn Light

## My Magical Pony

How would they find safety? What would Shining Star do?

The magical pony felt the rise and fall of the swelling waves and saw that the tide was full. So, carrying Krista safely on his back, he turned from the land, towards the sun in the east.

Krista took a deep breath as Star spread his wings and they rose from the water. They scattered shiny droplets into the air, flying higher and higher into the dawn light.

## Chapter Ten

As dawn broke, Jo and Rob followed Krista's mum and dad out of the back garden at High Point, across the field towards the wood.

"Krista must have brought out Spike's food," Krista's dad figured out. "Then she would call him to come and eat."

"Does he show up every time she calls?" Rob asked.

Krista's mum nodded. "Like clockwork. But if something went wrong and he didn't come, then she'd definitely go looking for him."

"But the weather was terrible and it was growing dark," Jo said. "So it's possible she soon got lost."

The others nodded. They entered the shadow of the trees, looking for signs that Krista had been there. A short distance away, a police helicopter flew along the coastline.

When the noise had faded, Krista's parents began to call their daughter's name.

The only answer came from the dripping branches swaying in the morning breeze.

"She's not here," Jo said quietly, after the four adults had searched the wood. They came out at the far side, on to the steep slope leading to the sea.

# Dawn Light

"Here comes that police helicopter again," Rob warned.

They stared up at the whirring blades, waiting for the roar to die down.

"She can't just have vanished!" Krista's dad muttered, striding on down the hill. "People don't disappear without trace!"

Rob glanced uneasily at Jo. "Sometimes they do!" he said under his breath. "Tragic accidents happen, especially at night!"

Jo closed her eyes and shook her head. When she opened them, she was the first to see the small grey moorland pony steadily approaching from the east. Only Krista could see the wonder of Star's wings and his beautiful shimmering mist.

"Look!" Jo called to Krista's parents, pointing to the wild pony that carried Krista towards them – a miracle at dawn!

"Don't hug too tight!" Krista pleaded.

First her mum and then her dad had flung their arms around her. She was still aching in every limb and her head hurt.

# Dawn Light

"Are you OK?" Jo asked, holding on to the wild pony while Krista slid to the ground.

"Stiff," Krista complained. "And cold."

Rob took off his jacket and wrapped it around her shoulders.

"Krista, we thought we'd lost you!" her mum sobbed. "It's been the longest night!"

"I didn't know anything about it," Krista mumbled. "I must have been unconscious for I don't know how long!"

Her dad said they must get her to the hospital. "Concussion has to be checked out," he insisted, picking her up and carrying her up the hill towards the house. "And they'll need to X-ray you to make sure you haven't broken anything."

Too weak to protest, Krista caught sight of
Jo leading Star. "He found me on the beach!"
she told them. "Without him, I wouldn't have
made it."

"What happened?" Jo asked. She stroked
the grey pony's neck and head.

"I don't know exactly." Carefully Krista
chose which bits to leave out and which to
explain. "All I remember is, I fell. When I
came round this morning, he was there.
I climbed on his back and he carried me up
to the top of the cliff."

She didn't mention the ghostly voices
that had woken her or the magical flight from
the depths of the sea. She would never tell
anyone the secret of Shining Star!

# Dawn Light

"Wonderful!" her mum sighed.

Star walked quietly beside Jo.

"You're a fantastic fellow!" Jo told him. "And so tame. I could almost take you home with me to Hartfell!"

"Oh no!" Krista cut in quickly. "He doesn't belong in a stable. He likes to be free!"

Everyone nodded and smiled. They were still discussing the moorland pony when they crossed the field and reached the garden.

"Hey, just a minute, look at this!" Rob exclaimed as he opened the gate. He stood aside to show Krista a solitary little spiky figure sitting patiently beside his two empty saucers in the middle of the lawn.

"Put me down, Dad!" Krista gasped.

She walked unsteadily towards Spike. "You're back!" she beamed, going down on to her hands and knees.

The hedgehog cocked his head and fixed his beady black eye on her. *What's the big deal?* he seemed to say.

"I'll drive Krista to hospital in my car," Krista's dad was telling Jo in the kitchen while her mum took her upstairs to change into dry clothes.

# Dawn Light

Rob had gone into the living room to call the police and tell them the good news. While he was there, the phone rang and he answered it.

"I'm so glad it's worked out," Jo was saying. "Rob and I would never have forgiven ourselves ..."

"Don't think about what might have happened," Krista's dad interrupted. "As you say, it's all worked out fine."

"Except that we still have to leave!" Krista sighed as she came back into the kitchen. Even her magical pony couldn't alter that. A glance out of the kitchen window told her that Star was still standing in the field at the back of the house.

Saturday, Sunday … the countdown grew shorter!

As Rob called her dad to the phone and her mum made her put on a warm jacket, Krista saw Shining Star turn to leave. "Everyone wait! I want to say goodbye to Star!" she gasped.

But before she could step outside, her dad came back wearing a look of total surprise. He shook his head, like a boxer who has just taken a crunching uppercut to the jaw.

"What?" Krista's mum asked.

Her dad stood in stunned silence.

"That was his new boss on the phone," Rob explained. "He told me it was urgent."

"What was?" Krista insisted, going up to

her dad and tugging at his arm. "Tell us!"

He shook his head again then cleared his throat. "It's about the job," he began.

"Oh no, you haven't lost it?" Krista's mum gasped.

"No. Listen. You know that the reason I got the sack in the first place was that my old boss couldn't make a profit. Well, this new boss got to hear about the situation and earlier this week he started discussions about buying the Whitton business."

"From your old boss here in town?" Jo asked.

Krista's dad nodded. "So they talked it through and that's what happened. My old boss is going to sell out to my new boss.

Now the new boss is on the phone asking me if I want to stay in Whitton and help put the business back on its feet."

"You mean, stay here?" Krista's mum asked.

Krista looked from one to the other.

"Well, do I?" her dad asked her mum and Krista. "Would you rather stay here or go to Bristol like we planned?"

There was a pause. Krista's hands flew to her mouth.

"Stay?" her mum asked her.

She ran to them both and hugged them in spite of her bruises. "Ouch!" she yelped. Then, "Yes! Yes! Yes!" she cried.

\*

# Dawn Light

"Did you have anything to do with that?" Krista asked her magical pony.

She'd run outside while her dad had gone to talk again to his boss and tell him that they wanted to accept his new offer. She'd explained what had happened with the brightest of smiles.

"I may have magic powers, but the ways of your world are not mine," Shining Star replied mildly.

"You mean, you didn't help with the job?"

The pony shook his head. "The news makes you happy?" he asked.

"Totally!" Like the sun coming out from behind a dark cloud, like the dawn light breaking and bringing Star to her rescue!

"I am glad," he told her.

"It means I can help Jo and look after the ponies for as long as I like!" Krista sighed. She looked into the future, and it was golden. "It means I don't have to say goodbye to you!"

"But I have to leave," Star said quietly. There were others who needed him in Galishe. He spread his wings. "We *must* say goodbye."

Krista nodded and smiled. She looked up at the magical pony as he rose from the green field. "But not for ever!"

"No, not for ever," Shining Star agreed, flying off in a silver cloud. "I will come again when you call."